The System

Simón Berrio-Ariza

Table of Contents

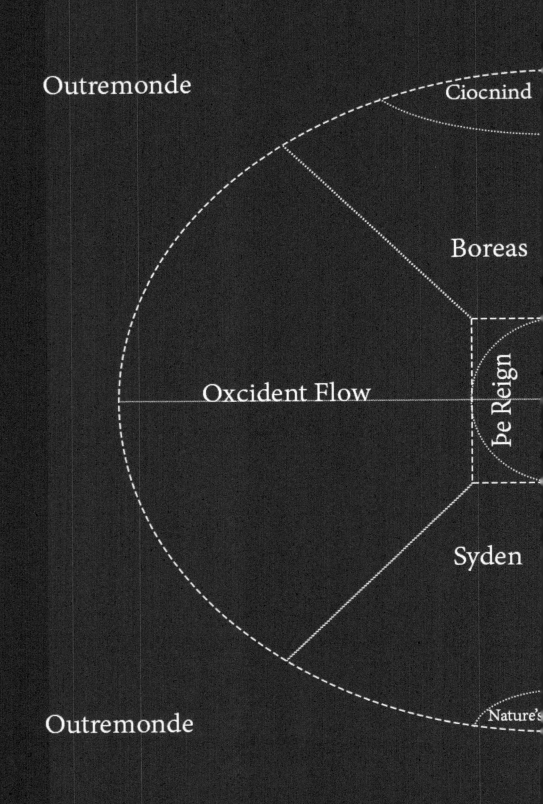

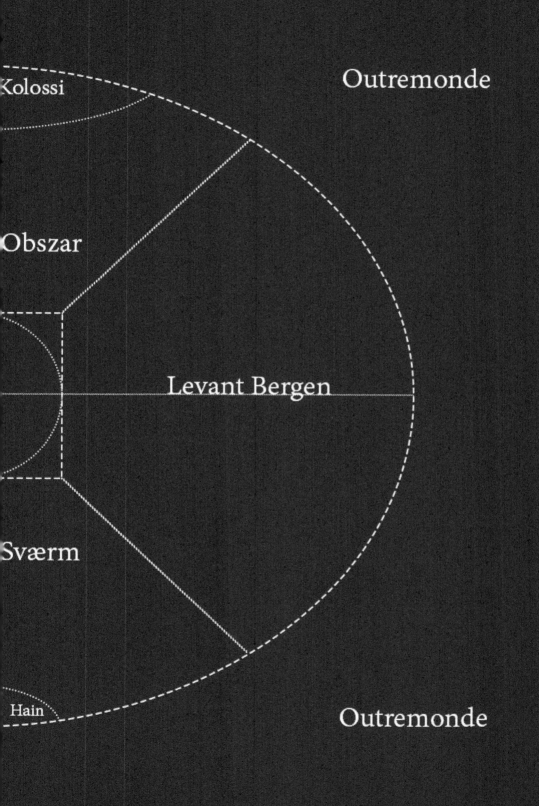

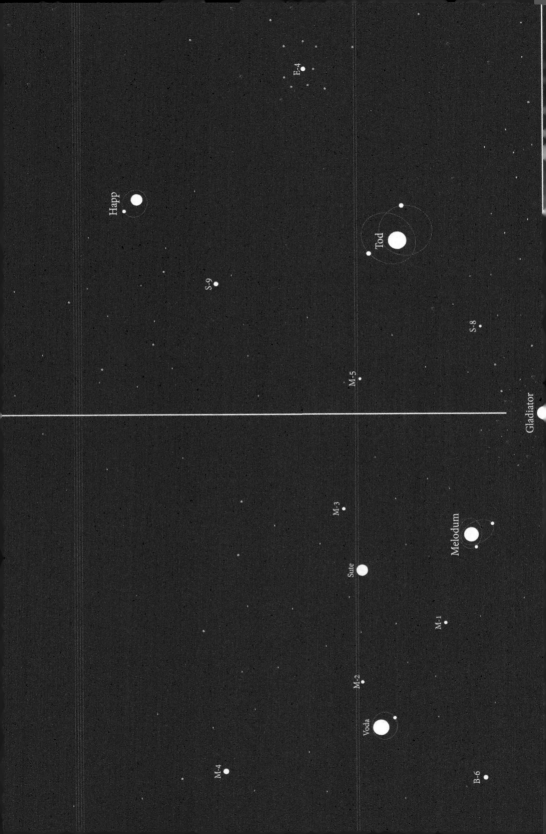

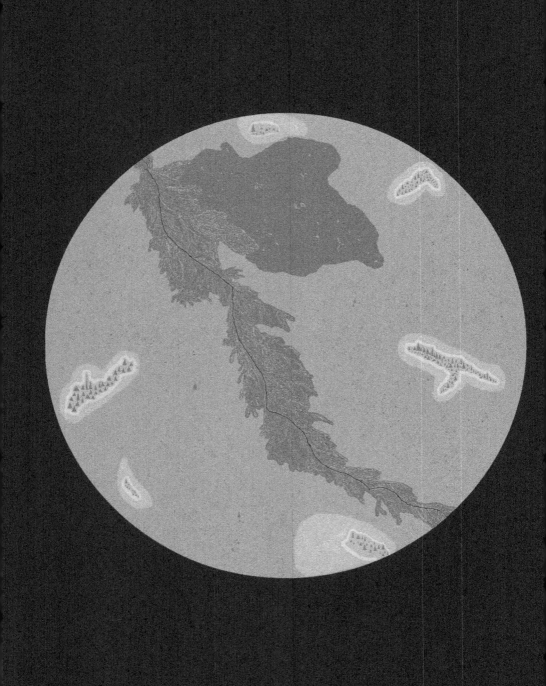

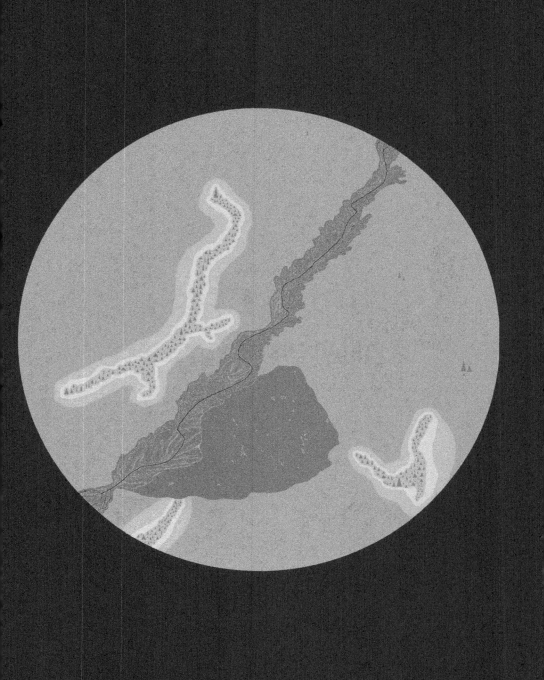

Inferences:
an Introduction

"Agog" Mung-Bai

This 376th: The definitive edition of "The System" by Thalon "Falcon" Yawn. I incite by my own part with a query; what should be proposed, what is pretended tobe, the purpose, the worth of poetry, and its begetter: the poet. In a world like ours or any other world, so intricate and expansive, fantasy itself may seem to lack the stature. Worse, even of unimportance in comparison. For 'twas and 'tis too well known, our NoF is an amalgam borne forth by an impressive fire-starting wreckage, then reforged by the hard work of untold eras 'n' ongoings, ending up with a union of phenomena, environs, as well life vastly obtuse and contrasting to one another. Truly, so numerous and differing, the majority would at first glance seem utterly unfit to suit each other.

However, strange things occur within song, space, and time. And from the most confounded disorder, mayhem, and chaos. Some order, as if drawn about by some numinous necessity, came about. That even though it may not concern thou or perhaps appears a frightsome cloud. The clevermost of the United Governance[1] whether a part of the "Fulcrum of progress & Exploration" (FPE)[2] or the minds at Artem & Ratio Solutions (ARS) guiding and leading the legendary ecumenopolis and Geniocracy of Eureka[3], tirelessly working at figuring this whole verse of ours out. Nevertheless, returning to the question: what role does a poet serve in this? If I were to ask some of the ancient and current, perhaps a similar answer, they would reserve and share.

---

1 Once independents, several species and governments were at odds for various reasons stemming from cultural, specieal, religious, ideological, operational, economic, and resource differences. However, the machinations and feats of the founder utterly changed that. In our history recorded under her moniker Þe Lull/Voïs', she nigh singularly begot the union. In its inception, she took the position of Þe Wise Seat in A.U. oF. The United Governance/U.G.: is a centralized governing authority of a super-imperial union of twenty formerly independent regional interplanetary organizations/empires/powers located and presiding o'er a majority of "Þe Reign" region of NoF, overseen equally by a twanomodictative regime, Þe Congregation of Humours and Þe Seat of Wisdom, respectively (colloquially known as the twenty and one). A single diplomat/representative from each of the twenty serves as a speaker for their people's needs, interests, and problems.
While the One, first fulfilling specific criteria, then passing an initial physical and mental aptitude test, undergoes an extensive series of trials and finally, by a majority vote of the Congregation, is selected as Þe Wise.

2 The Fulcrum of Progress & Exploration: one of several U.G. administrative arms created to increase integration between member powers and perform particular public service roles for the common welfare of the twenty and its peoples. Founded during the term of Wise. Wysheid (Served A.U. 2222F-2767F) though expanded upon since. Its function is to coordinate, supervise, and leads in its namesake while also regulating and directing one of the essential parts of the U.G. 's continuation and prosperity: the Reservoir Worlds. All this through its sub-organizations: Centers for Technological Advancement (CTA), The Expeditionary Collective (EC), and Management for Reservoir Worlds (MRW).

3 Eureka & ARS: Eureka is the capital planet of one of the member powers of the U.G. and is a central hub for scientific/artistic progress, experimentation, and excellence. Converted from a once naturally habitable globe to an ecumenopolis and complex that's possibilities and ability for adaption and reformation is and has long ever been beyond even the scope of the other wealthiest and strongest member powers, with perhaps the only exception being the sailing gas giants of the Thalassocracy of Loons. Artem & Ratio Solutions (ARS) is the governing body of the Geniocracy of Eureka, its worlds, and colonies.

"What dwells about our most pronounced To those impossibly hidden
The Yoll which conceives them"

From Yism I-1 by Qudssoon "O'Veils."

"Dearmost Ræys inspiring
Allow not the ink to fear me now
Let not the pen bore of my rhythms or clime
Keep the ichor mine misty
and as geysers spouting profusely
Upon each page spilling a warfield of emotion
Though that only ever the verses be laced   Encased in verity"

From The City O' Loons by Mackenroll "The Goon."

I feel a will has overtaken my soul
bearing along an ancient way
Which is to create
Bearing change as its result
happy as well to sacrifice for such an end
Even life and friends

From The Affairs of The Wind by Unknown.

Perchance 'tis nought more than empty and vague prattle on about spirits, volition, divinity, and so. However, I wouldn't have spent so long researching this text's history if I believed that, less even to try drawing up this intro for the work itself. Though true to note and merit holds to state. I've heard it all concerning a poet's work. Magniloquence or just some poor rhymesters drone on about some confused, manic, or melodramatic personal madness. That it'd be better in turn to drug up or institutionalize these woeful vagamonds than adhere, revere, or patron. For honestly, damned be my perchance "unscholarly" and largely expected tobe parti pris opinion. I dare to comment with some personal agree-ment. The more significant portion of the artistic issue now this day in age is less a need for open-mindedness.

Moreover, instead, the asylums need to be more prudent, active even, or better yet, more liberal with whom they accept into their catacombs. Of course, I'd implore not alone should poesy bear these critiques. All arts suffer from a litany. Abject mockery, insensitivity, disrespect, uncaring, poor education on the subject, at heart a prolific insouciance. Thus what do you expect of a culture or many ill-equipped to understand, internalize, or care? I signal out poetry because foremost, the book is a poetic work, and I question that the issue may also rest partly in a lack of discipline and a fundamental widespread gaining in cultural/societal indolence. I'll remark, from a viewpoint. It can take nothing to spectate; thou can witness dance, look at tapestries, watch films, listen to music haphazardly, and lackadaisically consuming these mediums. Though tobe able to enjoy or truly take anything from a text, one must-read. An action that takes some amount of investment whether time or study, or thought. Nonetheless, I am merely a scholar, just another of a multitude who recognize a malady and think they may have the solution though otherwise has neither the prestige nor genuine enough concern like a sociologist, activist, or politician to do something of it.

Back to the focus, to answer my own inquest. I will start with the principal character— Thalon of the dubbed illustrious, sanctimonious (insert self-flattery) lineage of Yawn. A minor though "notable" (as they'd all refer to themselves) Aristo-Gens originating from Timo.[4] Their claim to renown and prestige involves some progenitors in the long distant past, holding the office of Seat of Revelation in the Congregation of Humours[5]. Also, of course, sacrifice and bravery in the Apogean War[6] (Yet who does not have some brave ancestor that gave themselves to that horrid affair). They are currently insignificant in politics and are not even remotely involved with soldiering, spending their time enjoying the fruits of being wealthy landowning predatory beings as all do who are Aristo-Gens. Among the hierarchies of the Timoans, the Yawns are nominally considered the highest of the lowest, specializing in the administrations of vastly profitable ranches and plantations focus with a precious but limited number of factories producing unique, high-quality luxury goods primarily enjoyed by other Aristos in the various worlds controlled by Timo.

---

4 Timo/Aristo-Gens: Timo is the capital planet of one of the twenty-member powers of the U.G. Timoans, being the preeminent and sapient species. That at some point in the A.F. period of NoF before their ascension as a space-faring civilization. The powerful and capable of that era decided that through biological engineering and eugenics. They would uplift the varying species that their primordial ancestors predated upon—in turn, cutting out the weaker and "unnecessary" populations of their people. Therefore, creating a social structure and government called an ecosystemic aristocracy, a hierarchical system with themselves at the top and where the uplifted species are forever subservient. These lines/families chosen to persist and govern refer to themselves as Aristo-Gens.

5 The Seat of Revelation: is one of the twenty representative positions in the Congregation of Humours. "Surprise. (Insert Name)" being the title held by whom it is agreed to take the role. Selection for the occupation is completed by vote, moot, and competition among the qualifying Aristo-Gens on Timo and from other controlled worlds.

6 Apogean War/Age: A conflict lasting over eleven hundred Fet: A.U. 311-1423F or 4Y☒7T☒12F. It was between the United Governance and a power calling itself The Entente that rose during the Founding Age in direct response to the meteoric rise of the U.G. It ended with a total U.G. victory and a complete acquisition of all once-independent worlds belonging to the Entente.

Some of their products even reach as near as Bizalom's[7] worlds and ast far as Neart's[8]. That their general affair. While also basking in the popularity and revenue produced through the continuous publishings of this heralded work, whichs' reach has been U.G. wide, and occasionally copies and editions have made it to certain amicable exterior civilizations.

Now we touch upon the main dish. Though his Gens would negate reality and obstinately proclaim. Going so far as to claim conspiracy of defamation, threaten a lawsuit, or swift criminal punishment within their worlds, that Thalon was a beloved and cherished member of their Gens. So many reputable researchers, historians, documentarians, also just deeply invested fans have investigated the true nature of Thalon's relationship with his family. Discovering much evidence that such was not the case as they have claimed. It is still unknown when he was born that being of the least, what the Gens Yawn painstakingly tho' successfully erased, or perhaps that is biased; lost as is asserted. However, to describe to you the image of his youth. A normal ectogenesis to an at first joyous Gens, an education finest in his world, promising the future of political or military office somewhere. A hope, a light like any tyke when they are begotten and first learn. Nevertheless, sickness came, and sickness stayed. His whole life would be fraught, plagued as it were with unnumbered viruses, diseases, injuries, and the rest. Although never finding a final rest, if you will. Which cast aspersions and embarrassing rumors tobe set alight upon the Gens Yawn. Due to their inability to keep this one child in good health. To such a point, it impacted their trade, opportunity, and renown even. Which for them meant much embarrassment, eventually begetting shame and loathe. His forebears, ashamed of him, took him out of all limelight and, in many ways, just locked him away in their estates. Focusing instead upon the rearing 'n' tutelage of Thalon's siblings as well other youthful relatives. Though it would seem a dark star lorded o'er their line. Because many of Thalon's kin found their end by those very same varying maladies that had plagued tho' not taken him. His Gens, incapable of understanding how, who was considered the runt, the chagrin was able to survive. In due time, had him secretly (Keep in mind his practical disappearance from public life at their hands) Returned to certain laboratories of theirs largely presumed tobe their particular Omphalos-Auto[9], then tested upon, studied, and experimented with;

---

7 Bizalom: the capital world of one of the twenty-member powers in the U.G. that's original preeminent and sapient species, the Rukkhergians/Rukkherians. Its government is a Mache-theocracy following The Fide uf Mann/Fait ef Wyf. Led by two official balancing powers, the Empyrion w/the priestly class and then The Ordin uf Espeikons and their most extraordinary warriors, the dubbed Manns. With a third unofficial unorganized group of personalities holding more public than political influence, the dubbed Sans.

8 Neart: the capital world of one of the twenty-member powers in the U.G. Its government is a Military-dictatorship with naturalistic tendencies and peculiar institutions. Its majority species and people are the Nuvo-Stræng. Itself and its worlds stretch far into the eastern reaches of Þe Reign, reaching the border with The Levant Bergen.

9 An Omphalos-Auto is the womb of an Aristo-Gens; in esse, an advanced pangens study and manipulation multiplex used to bear the succeeding generations of a Gens. It is where Thalon was born and would have the equipment, scientists, and ability to research and discover the odd circumstances that had been occurring to him. More than this, it would prove whether it was a coincidence, a unique trait, or a flaw in their Gens Omphalos, which, if it had been the case, would have been a dire scandal. That requires immediate remedy for the discovery of a malfunctioning Omphalos-Auto and could prove to have devastating and even as far as deadly consequences brought upon them by other Aristos.

eventually to find out that Thalon had a gift that explained his survivability. He was born with an utterly rare mutation nought entirely unknown to the citizens of the U.G. and certainly dreaded one of horrid hexing immortality. Particularly for him, e variant of it allowing the mind and those parts that grant cognizance to go unhindered. The body, in the majority still able to feel pain, aches, and whatever else. Ergo explains the afflictions that afflicted his life. His bod' could decay and die over time, given a rather lengthy amount of time.

However, the consciousness, unless by suicide, will persist. Truly, that was the luck right there that he could choose his death instead of other famed cases. How did his flesh survive those pestilences as opposed to becoming whatever a bodily conscious is? Truly it could only be marked down as a case of perhaps the treatments. Daresay sheer will and hunger for life perhaps, helped push him into health at his most dire. He wished his carnality to keep on; thus, he kept it. Who knows the particulars of history? However, wouldn't making guesses be conjecture on my part? For those not so well versed in this, I understand. Immorality is an exceedingly uncommon happening. It all stems from a quirk/alteration of one's Pangens[10]. Coming about by certain pressures put upon offsprings (Differing in every species and unknown for most) during several or a singular point in the time of impregnation, gestation, to even close before birth. The emergence of this alteration is not so well understood, but what is known is that in every individual that it appears in, the phenomenon will be expressed uniquely; some are bound to live eternally while also relatively impervious to physical harm, yet some live infinitely but do age. The bod' becomes decrepit and useless while the mind will go on forever, or there have been cases of vice versa, with an undetermined amount of permutations or possibilities, but I will not go on. Recall, of course, I am a mere literary scholar, not some genius of Eureka studying limits of knowledge.

Now Thalons records after this are quite more scattered and uncertain. Supposedly the Gens, out of desperation, decided that perhaps new climates would aid the ability to bring about proper heirs. Thus there are bills of sales, titles traded, showing rapid asset acquisition and exchange with an ultimate relocation to an unknown elsewhere. Eventually, by their means, imps were created and raised to the proper age, and less and less is mentioned of Thalon in any memoir or note. During this time, what has been gathered from what evidence there is. Is that he was, in general, still viewed as a stain upon reputation and overall a bother. There is tobe something of heated arguments, debates between elders and himself. An odd predominance or maybe rather craze about letters and writ. A proposed union, then an Oath of Espeikon taken by someone important[11], followed by death.

---

10 Pangens: fundamental integrants of every living creature. To surmise, these hold, replicate, mutate, transfer, and build the diversity and necessary biological information, passed down through the untold/unnumbered generations of differing beings in NoF.

11 These events, by many scholars, are considered utterly uncanny. Due to the immense effort underwent to erode all information about who was involved in these seemingly climactic occurrences in Thalon's life. However, to give a little more general information. The oath of an Espeikon is a lifelong affair after its utterance. It promises opportunity and prestige beyond belief for the stalwart and unstoppable as they go from being a Tyke to full acceptance into the Ordin as a Guy. I mention this because the underhanded murder of any inducted Espeikon of any rank is a wholly ruinous affair. The culprits would suffer obliteration of themselves and their assets, executed either by tha victim's peers or mentor.

Further intensifying kerfuffles here or there, and a perceived odd proclivity of increasing interaction and celebration from Thalon to/with the subservient species of Timo[12]. Finally, a note from himself declaring his departure also affirms most of what has been found out.

To the Yawns,

I am the sound muzzled,
        A captured wolf whose howl is stifled.
    Bound to life,
yet to the world as inert ast any corse.
        And byn whom should I be kept?
        I've heard the question begged.
        For neither parental figures nor kin wish me theirs,
    or better still,   have the gut to put me dead.
Thus I hope once you find it.
    This simple parchment whose words I've hid within,
        for too long a time from youth.

        Through love that taught me more than any renowned tutor or chide.
          Till now,
after they who was lost byn thy conspiracy.
Cause well enough weren't them of your fancy.
        (However I never was also)
Couldn't you have been just estatic.
Myself stolen away where none couldst eye.
Taken flight ann new name,
gone off away.

        Nonetheless I quit festering the worst injury.
        I've pilfered thine coffers,
           taken what suits and shall carry me.
        Though don't think I will abandon yee.
Wheresoever I traverse what madness I confess to commit.
My name is from thee,
    Yawn and yawning forever I shall be!

After this began the longest-lasting portion of his life, wherein things alas become even hazier. It seems though he traveled using the wealth and name of his Gens assumedly by no small act of thievery, possibly through incessant ransoming of a particular essential item or through a consistent perennial theft of their digital assets. In truth, there is proof to suggest both were the case at some point or another. Now, as for what he did, there is evidence to suspect found in scattered documents and rumor, in general hearsay and from multiple interviews that have resulted in proving he had done something of a wrapa-

---

12 Fraternization between Timoans and their servant species is highly taboo. They are welcome to interact how they see fit, seeing as, of course, they rule. However, Thalon's people hold them-selves to various codes of conduct that especially disallow/stigmatize too much familiarity with the servile species.

round visiting and living for a time in the various worlds of each of the twenty-member civilizations of the United Governance. Where specifically and whom he associated with during this time is primarily unknown. We go off a multitude of scattered documents and disorganized claims. It is known for sure; eventually much aged, he returned to his Gens. Whether there was some reconciliation is alas not known.

Nevertheless, he did stay with them after all, having outlived his original Gens. Never himself having any romantic or legal union with another Timoan of his Gens or another, not even autosexually engineering an offspring in their Omphalos. He dearly cared for and advised the newer generations of the Yawn Gens, becoming relatively well respected by his distant nephews and nieces. Till at a point when he was very advanced in eras, he sat down and wrote this "The System." From what has been gathered, this was to him many things that I will not spoil. Yet what can be said is that to some extent, it was an oddly structured personal journal or maybe even just an organized collection of his ideations.

Eternity is a heavy burden. Such 'tis often conjectured that Thalon must have felt it did not suit him or anyone to keep on to view all the annals of ever, becoming wise as time yet burdened by decay that never had a fin to which arrive. Thalon did not publish this work, and whether he would have wanted or meant, who knows. His Gens found him dead. Truly a shock that must have been the immortal being found deceased. Nonetheless, they looked through his things, found the work, and didn't publish it, keeping it secret. Though it wasn't until some time later that someone I would call a hero did.

Thalon Yawn thus surveyed, explained, and rebounding now to the thesis again. Why must the poet be allowed their enounce? What use is a bard, troubadour, songster, skald, rhymester, or songbird? They are selfish bastards, a lot of them arrogant and lost. Nathless it is precisely that, life and nature so immense. They are so lost cause they can perceive it for what it is and believe it what it should be. All the life they take in: every corner, every crevice, every star, every urchin, behemoth, and forty winks they experience; they will spend an endless amount of instants rambling and gamboling about those simplicities. Transfixed, then into song transform, and word will turn these to things most would never believe. That a brawl between drunkards is the bout of two titans. Muscles glistening and fury as hath never been felt anywhere. Cloud the very air, stealing all ability to breathe.

Then when one falls fat and heavy, provoking an earthquake that shatters continents and a'last that very same one lets out a blech that blows the whole bar down in a tornado. Poetry is madness put to order by song and rhythm; poetry is the mystics' preference and the centerpiece of his magic. Poetry is the quotes of sages; Poetry is wind evermore blowing freely, purring wildly into the ears of those with eyes to witness, ears to listen, hands to have it written. Poetry is ardor, loath, and miseries only valid means of confession; poetry is the word of divinity, taken solely from what has anything to do with such a meaning: soul. If nature itself be trilling, the poet is the vehicle, the mouthpiece to that singing. They account for all the world and leave nothing sans being spoken. No matter the plenitude of insanity. All of it shall be warped, transformed into words of horror, truth, and beauty.

One does not ask the monster why it does what it did. For the beast's acts speak. These are words; these are verses, I shan't explain rhythm or style, that, thus, or this. As we hoped he wanted, I'll let it have its tithe.

18

The System

Thalon Yawn"The Falcon"

Dedication.

This goes out to my kind
The wild beasts   the wild dames
The violent   the rough
          the kind   the caught
                    the basterds   the buff
          The secretly gentle   the willful blind

To those who knew me

And those who tried

Fusion.

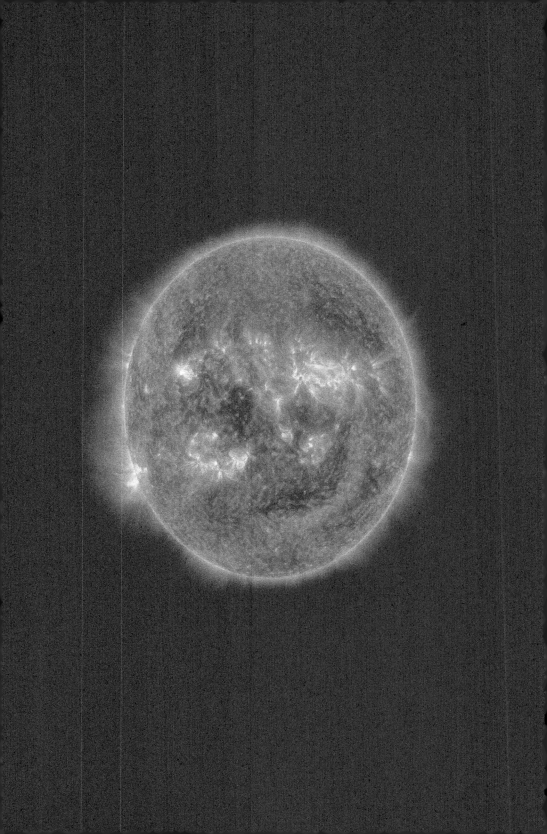

I have thought
So I am begun

There's a buffoon in the distance
amid reaches continents 'n' deeps
They speak now whispering

I am Thalon Yawn

Not my choice sure enough
but like a toy or mutt
That's the name I was taught
So to it   It alone I'll respond
Now don't count me vexed for my luck
Don't believe presently I'm anything like a down n out yup

Just hear out my writ
I have quite a bit to split

And dear Amadio[13] do I mean it, don't think me cross
Cause coincidentally that'd make me real stark

Now I have all the controls currently
So when you imagine who I was
think as thus
I'm a titan and a hero   some sage
and why not o   wise vagamond
A monster in plain sight
but with the camouflage of forgot
E terror from nowhere with good ol' lacertilias regenerative prowess
Yet I wouldn't like to make things up
or give a bad impression to whom I share this correspondence
I was never more evil
never most saintly
Then that time we saw another suddenly
Passerby   was it the sidewalk
O perhaps you spotted me   Me in my vehicle as I blasted off
Did you contemplate me every time ya spied
Yet just always felt content on the watch
Uur was that me

---

13 Amadio/Amadio Lator: is the professed head/progenitor of a race of deities dubbed the "Wer/ Mann. These are the gods of the "Fide of Mann," a widespread religion in NoF originating from Bizalom. Like other civilizations, ex. Deplin, Neart, Krig, and Nalfa, by the time of Thalon, Timo's native species had mostly or entirely converted either by diplomacy or force.

It's difficult isn't it to start up abruptly with a new someone
But no that's not the muck
'Tis quite easy togo up to them then say "Ole what's up"
Rather and dare I to strike as such
(Pardon fate being called)
We wert never meant to talk
No sequence no order no formula that equated to us
At least not farther than gawks gazes glances or offhand remarks
However that much we are blessed to share
So lemme recant to you how I really am was or will be once this is done
That lardo or twig
funny face   broken brain
Hot one   or yuck
The I should go up to her
The come on   he's got to come to me
The one you laugh at for falling
O that one
who said good morning in the afternoon and vice versa
Mister random eye contact
and madam digging for gold when they think none are looking
The one you wonder where his head is at
The one ye think "She's a loose one"
The one who answers all the questions 'n' always asks them
Know-nothing   Know-it-all
In the back   against the wall   or at the fore
That misanthrope who nearly got you killed for having been an idiot
Yet also
that swell character whom you spent hours amicably conversing with
Though in the end never catching their name
Never asking for some point of contact to reach them again

Such said 'nd I don't mean to boast
I'm everyone of them
even more also
But can anyone describe each probability
Ann now don't leave yourself out of these odds 'nd ends
For I can recall one through ten continued on howsoever long the list gets
Thou thee 'n' thy were one of these at some time

Done with me let's talk of what I am todo currently

So for you who looks presently
I pull forth 'n' pool before thine peepers
Amalgamating   Wrenching together
A vision
I will build for you a system
This I can for having been a witness
And tho' you may find to just hold tha ideas in derision
Thus be it   I'm understanding toward suspicion

I want to bring then deliver
To your clearest view (Kin of effulgence I'll aspire)
revealing what cognition made up my spirit

Coming naked   Loosening my orifices
A revealing
we've done that for someone haven't we
'Nd that's wondrous. (Well unless you're empty or shallow
then what will one be looking at
A pity)
Taking down the crucifictions
Of living as hermits within bustling scenery or cities
(Easiest thing)...

By spell so-to begin

✴✴✴✴✴

Yellow starts with the sweetest taste
It glows iridescent
and rends away the darksome cascade
O
Grinding teeth   and jaw bones lock
Muscles tensing   the crick is sharp
Only let pour   necessity

Wreck rummage ruination break
Convulsing calfs 'n' melting biceps ache
Feeling pain   so alights tha drawing closer uf age
The entities away are arriving in haste
Readying clubs for bod 'nd grey
Onlooker   Stranger   Peculiar
I call at you to escape

"SHATTER"

Relief and a sigh   Now we go-on the ride
Purely cleansome come along on the raft right next to I
Yellow first will try
We start our sailing in an amber sky
Riding over an aureolin ocean
With gold lands behind   sunglow ones aside   jonquil islands beside
In this goldenrod boat quicked by maize sails
Ann gamboge decorations making it a wonder to eye
Chewing mustard to keep us astir
Got hay in wheels to sit upon
A dream full of lemon lime and jasmine
This is where we come together
Wearing ecru silks
eating apricots to be filled
For this ride is long

Combining   getting mixed in   coalescing ain't an easy state
It's hard to speak out when everyone's talking
Can't be an individual if everyone tries so hard tobe one
That's exactly the action which makes us unimportant
Having too much self-importance
Goodly numbers one can count as they travel rounds
I wonder how high that'd be   the account I mean
If we numbered all those who we never just tried   reaching out on our going bys'
*****

Of subjects millions one could spout
But here I'll go with only those I feel count

Lo alchemy what can I whirl
To concoct and brew
in the cauldron wrought forth an improbable stew
You see in my transfiguring pan
I will chuck in some guts   some will   some fear
Sprinkle some dear   some daunt   some leer
Then from these we shall form some form anew
E brand new peer
one we have nothing todo with but a tear

Lonesome and dearest are the alchemical studies and durst
We each are a work
a mixture of supple 'n' coarse
Thank the gravities for drawing those progenitors together
Whether one or several
Thou is comparable to a test for in forming you
The struggle couldst be unbearable
Some take their lives for less stress
(What does that say of the limits people have)
Now there are bad alchemists and the good
Speaking not of morales but of quality in care
Some create then forget   Some make and mistreat   Others begot but overbear
Many are quite terrible at creation and craft
But that's just due to history continuing sans a smack
We're never best at being direct
Working with any odd and end or advantage or crack or bend
Whatever eases the trial
of ensuring thy potion doesn't end as another poison
Instead rather a fresh uur rare elixir to upend/correct what's at hand
Though can we only think of those initial indolents idiots or masters that we've had

Never
For by many claws jaws palms   Or feet
Whether by droves or lones
There are many   if solely within one moment or o'er an entire lifetime
Have spent their instants building upon the brew that is you
A magic trick   Some little lesson
E maxim   E message
Sex drunkenness friendship vitriol   Being dense
The constant interactions
A tid or bundle of each wretch   of each blessed
Taken from themselves their own extract or esse goes into yee
The incessant turns taken   spinning the spoon
Evenly churning those freshly added ingredients with the already pleasantly colored broth
Always things being added never lessened
Nothing can grow or improve without something different impressing
Now can we admit it is all pleasant
Aren't sometimes too many things placed upon us
A horrid herb or ruining spice thrown at we
Maybe a crippling some distraught and there we go almost totally ruined
Well the question then is did you survive its addition
For such things even them can be blended making a concoction much tha better
Nothing totally would destroy unless it taketh away
For when a thing is stolen once it'll happen more
And the many times around galore
Wouldn't be the same no matter how much you implored
In these happenings one has to find the right thing to equal the damage with healing
If a building collapses before its builders
They can complain they can feel vex and rude
They can discuss   what if that perhaps could have prevented such
Yet nonetheless from scratch again they'll have to contest
By hope a little wiser from the prior mess
So
never the preparation is it finished I would say
Till perhaps that day or dark
Upon which we art relieved of our tread and bed
Life itself tasting our blend   a whole serving   a blissful glassful we can hope
Drinking us deep
As we ourselves are spread about plains or deeps
And if we were truly the draft conceived tobe
Though we shall never see the results
Those who continue sure will
Some even carrying us
our drink nurturing their own

Now of a sister topic
Similar though distinctly apparent
Art artistry magic
Have thou seen the majesty of a tapestry
Of recanted histories through jovial tunes
Bashful muse and abrasive youth
An elders requiem a young one's sighing
E song or painting displaying some new apprehension
What is it
Intaken be the horrors 'n' tha beauties
Within the body deeply dranken
and there in the furnace of that stomach
Transfiguring then releasing
Another way to simply display it
Imagine eating   meat   leaves
water 'nd beans
Down they go
reaching the bottom of your hole
Pooled below in o mass of mashed slop
Yet next suddenly it glows
Heating sweltering broiling
Transformed a perfect crystal borne
You struggle for it shakes
Quaking like some tectonic plate at the break
Slowly inching out till abrupt its shot up
Your face is forced to point above
Thy mouth opens
'n' the bijou rises forth held there by the bite of thine jaw
There such a thing begins to crack e little
Enough to allow a dragonfly from inside to get through
Succeeded by a butterfly last o wasp
The three beginning a waltz
Swiftly becoming a speedy ballet
Till pirouette
Gyrate
Gyrate gyrate
Spindle spinning and sudden flame
Each striking the jewel in fastest blaze
And LO the collapse of twilight 'n' day
Rises forth otherworldly beings from the gob
Beautiful and terrible
secret and impossible
They launch everywhere and how
To show all around
the pure quintessence of experience and esse

The soul poured in a work
Filling it to the brim of its flask
Be it page wooden floor canvas or other form
Only that is art
or can be what is worthy tobe of that class
Even a life can be so
I mean the only one worth taking part in
Is that kind which risks tests and brings joy to tha spirit

Last to tell for this bit   Is this
I ask thee
Where did that thing
that force or vitality (however to speak)
Beauty   from where did ist appear
From here
in words unspoken
Words only the nuclear could tell
'N' when it rose
How did it so
Well as all things grand I assume
With a BAM

Stranger to Stranger
Unknown to Unknown
Each other's vacuous familiar
Our times intertwined
I see us turning out
a different manner than when we espied one another on our rounds
How we shall opt now
Partners
Thus onward

Mercurial.

Resolution   Absolution   'n' Restitution
        Three line worked nooses
To find thrice ol' odds put upon us
        As these triplet dealers
                        Offering products to damn or free
                Will name them to give them a little personhood
Rez   Abe   'n' Rest
        Brother like merchants
                        that'll now each gift you their spiel

                Rez   Confidence in dilemma
        A wise choice in troubled straits
        Calculated decision making
                Obstinance and oh the foolhardy brave
                        Simplicity discovered after complexity
                        A return or come about to harmony

                Ergo the welcome turf after æons spent abroad upthere or in whirl

                Abe   Pardon and liberation
                        The blanket release of strangling sensation
                                Uncaring 'n' selfishness
                        Swagger 'nd sway sinless aldays
                                        The unbounding of instants gone passed by
                                A statement of guiltless living
                        E feeling nonpareil lifted in symphonic blairs
                Perhaps betrayal remedied
        what had chained the shared fresh air

                The crippling haunt of yester did away
        A phoenix healthily springing from the hardshipped egg

                Rest   Guerdon Ho Solatium
        Desire   Need   tobe respected for what you do
                Your damages injuries 'n' painstakes yielded to
                        Toil harshly spent   finds fruit
                                Patience 'n' providence
                The wait for some another time to arrive
        where another shall spend the moments for you

                The vista after sleepless dark
                        Horizon launching e lie-less inferno onto the sky
                                In a great parade of color 'n' untouched light

34

*****

Grey grise   Heia silver
    Gainsboro   platinum
         Gunmetal   taupe
Rose quartz marengo ann slate
We traverse the stream through the misty veil
Finding destiny nemesis fate
    the better things 'nd pain
    How does each of us play into the play
Happenstance and the colliding passions decide the dance
We art subject alone to our own acts
    Obscure us art to each other
A miasma or storm of reasons and plots
        Platitudes uur excuses
        Fantasies o ruin
    But these things are unknowable
for noone reveals all their holds fullness
*****

    So mostly lonesome
we sought ourn avenues or vertices from whence to penetrate in
    Find the place to inject 'n' infect
    Converting the situations into desire's true face
    But antibodies do respond
    Hardline cures to follow their assault
Routing acts and deeds
    Eviscerating all advances to one's dreams
    These are those others i speak of
    the litany
O random multitude
In such games as ours where everyone one presses forth
    Something always tries to return to the status quo
    Or instead press back upon you
    The unexpected occurrences
tha traitor's   te enemies   ta disasters
    yet not all are on purpose
Sometimes another decent person just happens tobe trying
    You e casualty of their ambition
Just like anyone   anything can be to yours

Fate what happens at ya
    Hark tha billion situations
Infinite misgivings   lies   derisions
perpetual amours   jubilees   'n' happy distractions

Eternity has in store for you a hurricane

Destiny equates to Decision
Split instant mistakes and victories
Weakness in testimony   Daring under inquiry
Trust   betrayal   energy   viciousness   generosity   and Discipline
Speaking through silence
Senseless berate
Melancholy   Practice   'N' wisdom even if we dare to say

Now those hordes I've spoken of
Uf which us both are members alongside

Where do they play in this ring
Each from their own corner
None other foe than you 'n' me
Of course and everybody else of who you could think
Those they don't know all too well or never met
Trillions of obstacles hidden right before their senses
As they motion through dark or light
through each wane 'n' wax of time
However few are truly alone to brave a whole
That is why we have perception
Muddling scouring through those we perceive   Deem 'em the plentitudes

Finding dear ones hither o thither
Special characters to keep near
Thus each soldier was the ally 'n' reinforcement of another

Lovers friends even family members
Consider though many are born and cared for by these special folks
That doesn't make them family or of import
It is neither right by birth or just so by impulse
Each being decides who is wondrous 'n' worthy tobe their peer
Strangest to say these three domains tend to interblend
Because any can take the place or be all in tha same

Nonetheless 'n' I digress
let us come once again to this topic I profess
Thy dole doom 'n' due
Each being 'tis a libertine till honed in by society's beating
Regulations law 'n' jurisprudence
Always in their most unfair of garbs
Attrition and cold retribution
(For can any rule truly be fair
If someone eventually gets the long irons   toughest stuff
Wrenched upon their bod
quelling and sealing they's knuckles toes 'n' head)
There truesome are meances and despotism
When life is stamped out as easily by a pen
as byn a plod with his bayonet
Is anything possible then

In such cases only a conscious is e refuge
The torturer and executioner behind the questioner
Playing roshambo to see who will get them's chance
To peel away sanity or drain from you thine vitality
So do we rebel when we're oppressed
But why fight
Forcause many a time repeating as if 'twere inescapable
Brave creatures with a torch alight byn swell intention
O the pretension of something must be bettered
Fo' themselves 'n' those they claim compeer
Ever these of such mindset
Surrender virtue o fine thinking
transformed by sore 'n' gore trial et galore
To the things once they wert agin
Such ta hold on fast
those changes perhaps so harshly gained
Tha deepest dread of losing what ya win
Due to the wanton and whims ef misunderstanding beasts or kin

Can we not all see ourselves like this
With such selflessness going on to commit grandiose deeds
'N' betrayed by those we acted for
in turn taking the most selfish course
to force

So day to day
Trying with little actions 'nd small taskin'
Togo about conducting oneself in accordance with the morale mass
Who is that
Well doesn't everyone want todo good by their peoples 'n' land
Hoping that through tender efforts or kind acts
Somehow the shear number amassing
turns about into a storm of nicety 'n' uprightness

However I see that aged wisdom
ef the far off paradise-like village
Uur singular warm-heart
beginning the swirls
Uf the grand upheaval of squalor or evil
Being undone throu just some mere opportunity
Tuu gain over their fellow any quantity
whether it a minor win or major victory
Betrayal o duplicity
ends one no better than the corrupted clergy
But who can criticize canst I
I'm one of these and do proudly vaunt
You yourself also
Yes   yes we are all saints n monks
Kindly souls gentle lugs
Altho' we art each other's great rival or pawn
The villain in each story or cruel for fun
Thou doubt surely enough
Thus when again you gain the objective you sought
Think how many others were left to suck it up
No intention held ya to screw o'er another
However ever remember your success cost someone else's
Truly be proud
though watch for the flair of arrogance
For along the road   you yourself could then be snubbed
By whom than that very unknown sighted once or never espied
I to you you to I
Circular life tends to round back by
It's one's own job to set the shape 'n' conclusion of their course 'n' cause
Ovals also circle

Now if but an itty indulge inta history
A tiny tome oxymoron I know
Cracked open from my mind's deep dungeon long unexplored

Its sticky webs   caked dust
'n' coagulated musk
resisted and dove through

Does anything ever repeat
Is learning ever truly a clean thing

Utilize your elders' experience
Learn another creature's lesson
Heed the master

Well to perdition with cliches
Perchance there's a reason wisdom is hard to convey
All mistakes have the allure to commit inlaid
And all wisdom comes from those who did not obey
Who questioned 'n' rebelled thinking it'd be different
Each great one who took the chance of facing folly
Matter not the failure or setback
No matter if it's dark or dread
Breeds forth a single gleam at every end
That hopefully
some loving soul could keep dear
Bringing with hope new joy into these worlds
Than such continuous melancholia

So whereof starts a revolution
Genuinely doth change ever spawn and wrought forth a new conclusion
Consistent unwavering once its won
Everything deemed to ebb 'n' raise
How can anything propose to transmutate
Predetermined   Mundane   samesame already explained

Guessing it's with a flair

Abrupt   Random   Inspired
          craze   raze   the wild
              Sudden motions
                    swift rebukes
                          standing for quick redresses
              Windlass the courage from the most fearful core
Launching then with the might of some rampart breaker
                    At the dread partitions withholding a goal
                          Slow the siege but swift the assault
                    'Tis only with keen desire
                          'N' a staunch attitude
              You realize a wish

              There is not savior or master to guide a mass
And you e part of it following with just glance at the one guidin' the path
                    Some meager gaunt all along nothin' more

    The individual is a tremendity
              If he she it allows tha self tobe
                    Want righteous leaders
                          Lead yourself
              To the foreground of the heaviest bout
          Follow the commands of thy psyche
                    fearless to the hammer and wrench
                          and protective of your hopes

                    Subject to...   What should you be
          Only that which wouldn't poison the volition to kneel
    A wise 'n' sturdy will earned its standing by daring deeds
                    More so than niceties or pleasantries
                          Find your keel 'n' keep it real
          For when it rots the whole ship shall keel

                    There are great powers
              Forces unhindered unimaginable
          Exercising themselves always unto thee
    Inevitability is how anyone's soul gets pinched 'nd yoked

Like the volcano
Once its call rings hearty
Its groans turned mighty
The final yawning vomit
What do all the elements do but listen 'n' come supporting
Typhoons risin"   Quakes convulsin'   Tsunamis cresting
Be like them
For none command ye then
Not even those you befriend   give alms
'n' love send

Vein.

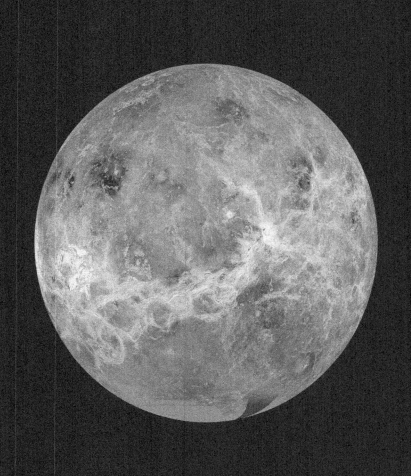

I made love to some divines
and they reduced me with a furious grind
Yet showed me scenes of serene things
Costing me all faculties I could once claim keen

The subject lets peer
Is nothing more dear
Than the will 'n' its kin
the blood within
I mean why else is it spilled

I saw the blood of a prodigal son
borne in purple and ready for hell
Green as a wet field
but ferocious as a scream in-held
Alas his handsome face was known too well
For when I saw disease
like a great fury overtake his bones
And the single instant that I recall
those first ichors I spied
escaping as he tried
Hiding his body's failings 'n' pangings
I recognized then at instant the oncoming tragedy
That would be wrought by his waning

Funniest thing to be undesired
Funny a thing to bury your prized child
Whilst the runt goes on living everon

What makes lifeblood a bond
Is it just where it comes from
No it's a different kind of blood
Different life essence
Different thing that ties
Familiar love
Kinship
and fostered heart
It is only that which ties two or a multitude to you

Is it also a lifeblood that makes one superior or weaker
The luck or fluke of having been born with certain peculiarities
Strengths
Capacities
Wits
Endurances
Manners
Weaknesses
Madnesses

Idiocies
Lackings
Worldly standings

Bad blood
Good
Pangen majority minority

Quality   Quantity

Just chances workings
That's the wonder of it
You who is ugly walking beside the pretty
Looked over n spat at
scoffed n rejected
Leaves a wight dejected

Nobles 'nd wealthy
ignorant and academia
Species crazed and obsessed o'er the little meaning in ethnicity

None yet born are more worthy
Nor those just come about

They can't be
for randoms such as me go forth out living
Go superseding
Go conquering our frailties
More durable by every disease we pass through
More power lies in this than the perfect Pangen stock inherited

Never havin' beared a cold
How does a whole people fare
With endless medicines
perpetual protections
Regulations boundless
Safeguards 'n' false achievements nonstop
I'd say for all the miracles of the current age
Safety is the least meritable
Makes a long hardened n hearty people
A bunch of braggarts indolents 'nd caitiffs
Forebears should be more weary of their endeavors 'n' inventions

They whose lost a little of their vital fluid
Be a paper cut or crushed foot
Have more to them
than the most cautious sheltered fool

Watch what you do to the youth
For your perfect little lineages
That Pangen collection making us of all colors 'n' do's
So witness as it makes you all inept

graceless
faceless
crippled
freakish
and stillborn

'N' why would you cry then
It was the ancestors doings
en yours too
If you fell for making stupid bets
Keepin on the adding scum to the already filled pond
Ya doing a good job
Lessening trivial pains
Ill-preparing youngings for the stars or fate
What'll they do when huge agonies come
Succumb
Give up
Hate
Let it all wash them by

Is a certain happenstance of your kind to be the source of pride
Or is it the accomplishments the whole band could devise
The overcomings trials n joys at last after everything unkind
The peace everyone could find
Something more valuable than what's noticed only in a glance

Blood lost is ever more admirable   respectable
than that you're given to start off

*****

Sways of amethyst
Sea quakes rising grape tsunamis
Purpureus sky full of violet cumulonimbus
Overcoming the æthers invading mountain chains
Descends from them a hail of irises
Alongside airs of a lilac 'n' lavender odor
Gusts carting about e million thistle n orchids
Joining into a mælstrom of tropical indigo
full of mulberries n wisterias
Sparks and bolts blasting about
with a machinegun's rate of fire
All an electric indigo uur other purple
En you upon thy raft an eminence
As the violet tides force   throws you up to the bow fore
A fandango unfurls
Such what happens next
With your pomp and power straight at the whirpool you dove
No pansy tobe found
the utter cornerstone no doubt
Of us ultras upon this redoubt
*****

Such is the key to victory
Willing things tobe
Let your charisma take hold
Convince others todo as you would propose
Uur if thou are lacking   use your force
Impose not ideas but goals
Nothing gets done throu' letting it go or leaving tobe
At that point just leave
Dance bravely around violence 'n' bad humors
Although never be fearful of direct action
Crush an annoying fool in thine palm
Blow the enemy away with an exhale off the tongue

Ahh however nature opposes
The grander forces are thy shoulders
Well do you not control breathing
Is not air or some aqueous thing
itself a mandatory for your being
If 'tis not   is some other element core to your spirit
Anyways   use it today
Anything can be defeated
Stubbornness well is a virtue
Even if many would disagree

46

If the world is obstinate
    Why should you give ground
        Unless that is
            thou found a hidden path to sally forth on mount
            The advantage is a quick instant clasp
                A fountain uf luck found

            Volition
The motions produced by a souls exploding 'n' growing
        Act
            wait not for roads to show
        Momentary pausing to better sight the options
            Wonderful
            Though never forget
            movement must resume
      Uur others will stir where you were hoping
        It is in those times our resolves tested
          You decide whose tobe bested
        "Nonetheless they outmatched me"
      Only due to your lack of attention
    Few things truly come from nowhere
      For little are we truly unprepared
          Everything had an option before it happened
          The rounds 'n' routes eternal
    Is screwing up or slipping   an excuse

      The wet lifeblood is drying on the fighter's body
          Covering their scars
        sealing wounds
      coating their enemy o rival
    The skin I can't see
      Dirt clay sand mixing
        a beast hurting yet fighting
          No freckles no moles
            No warts no wrinkles
          No smoothness no dryness
        A raw heart pumping
      A raw body gushing out
    Fresh gore envieling everything
      Energies exposed
    I see choice drive 'n' mind
  Out freely in flow onto the sky
  Then the next punch is thrown
Tha next sword swing swung
  Spear shaft stuck
    Bow shot hit its mark
      Gun fire blast apart

Mace rock its wreck
Lasers burn through
Plasma melts all
Grenade booms shrapnel zooms

When you fight to live
(Same as for it)
There is nothing too cruel too rude
Do for you 'n' yours what ya have to
Costs are costs
only one really has to bear 'em
'N' that's whom it came down to
Whatever they are ye made the moves

So live with them
Don't be regretful buffoon

Enkindle.

Effulgence rise
      Supernal extremities combine
         If we find
            the lasting marks of a serene time
              Tobe so bland we capsize
            Then almighties and divines
                may yee strike us all
                    With awesome clouts
                      Full of molten metals ensnared
                    in fantastic infernos of mulithued fire

             Wherefrom art dreams begot
        I speak of nachallucins nought
          Those their nature remain ever a mystery
        But of wish need or want
          Them are my talk
     Uf ramparts taken by the brave and villainous
Perhaps risin' to the zenith of thy line of work
      Traveling the streams 'n' seas where I hear the gleams glow happily[14]
        Traversing the wild ranges 'n' horns higher than height
             full of nothing known waiting an explore[15]
    Risking through impassables miasmas fogs and mists
        Where one couldnst see fore or fathom bleak[16]
    Going elsewhere instead whereso none yet have espied or tried
Where resourcefulness and maintaining your brawn win ya more time[17]
          Beating a beast down   Terrorizing a town
    Revenge Love   Fight   Peace   Prize
          Chasing little lillies fleeting by
            Catch all you can
            For all the others about
          will gather all those you'd desire

---

14 Refers to the Oxcident Flow of NoF lying west of Þe Reign, where there are æther currents resembling rivers and seas. They are composed of atmos, solar wind, plasma, and gas. They are perilous to navigate for their propensity to change direction abruptly.

15 Refers to the Levant Bergen lying east of Þe Reign, where the constant shifting movement, destruction, and reforming of celestial mounts, utterly dense asteroid/debris fields, and other factors make it a danger to cross and explore.

16 Refers to the Syden Sværm located south of Þe Reign and completely unexplored for its impassable miasma that, upon entry, instantly begins to deteriorate almost all known materials and, of course, does well to bring about first madness and eventually death to any sorry living being passing through it.

17 Refers to the Boreas Obszar, which lies north of Þe Reign, marked by a seemingly large, predominantly empty expanse. That does contain some rogue worlds with their varying inhabitants sparsely located. At the extremities, there are violent roaming dwarf/giant worlds made entirely of gas or other matter that art constantly shrinking, growing, colliding, and separating in the northmost reaches.

Thus ye end up within e gyre
Caused by the swivels n speedy motions of better persons like
With nothing worth a tithe of squawk o pride
When wing is taken
Do you hesitate   Do you die away
The airs at you
you must reciprocate
Maneuvering   using the bluster and pound
uf gust 'nd squall
Slyly n suspicious watching the zephyrs
Their trickery always at arms
Ready to fire with za full force of a howitzers volley
At once the boulders are launching
The sand in a devil coming
Fat waters in a torrent like power dropping
You meet it with a bolo and corkscrew
Roundhouse followed with a crescent
And as it cries a howl to bleed the eyes or ears dry
Pick up a flute or guitar
Better yet a drum
Beating to the beat of thine pulse
Harder and harder
Till thy sound scare off titan or law

Cease e chance with shackle en bind
Selfishly guarding as o hermit its peace or far off mountain hut
However not every one option is a fine luck
Several some trap uur loss
Mind your states mindly or otherwise
Mind where you've been and where you'll someday consider to have gone
Mind that rollick ann spin
Mind thou foe's Kin
passerbys their peer o leer
Advantages snags backtracks speedups
Each a scenario to revel 'nd clasp
Learning better from these   for victory at the next task

*****

I shall describe to ye this instant
The territory of bows n skylines we have found
Our dear rafts sailing has made it to this orange fount
A gigantic geyser mid the sea of mahogany
spouts forth a tangerine blast
While a ring of eclipses amber 'n' bittersweet encircle about staring down
Causing nacreous clouds tu turn a whole array of vermillion
gamboge carrot 'nd gold bullion
One pumpkin star though peaks out
Sun dogs appearing forthwith
their barking changing them from coral to persimmon
We see the parhelic circles shine jonquil and peach
Horizons far away ef butterscotch of flame
Doing a wave like dance
To honor tides lion strong
Thus we ride with caramel skin
Tangelo cheeks   Tea rose hair
Peach-orange eyes
Champagne in our bellies
And scarlet palms
Raw from trial ann trek
Seashell blisters popped
bleeding out rust
But still these hands
art ready to be assayed

*****

Is there more to reveal
free-spoken and sweeting
Ast a wolves stare
no matter if held by manacle
uur behind some barrier
Unrestrained
Stark

For aye unbroken

Moor.

What lungs do we prefer
Filled with regular gusts
intaken too often
Their taste all too felt
Of settlements and theirs boroughs
Lavish homes to their brims with things
The average everyday locality
Unexplorable   understood in its totality
From a ornate corner view
Comfortability too much o commonhood
Sitting there e'er   unmoved
the enforced policy   tallywho

But nostrils   skin   throat
They call with rancor 'n' beg

Tobe full of breeze from distant territories
Untouched regions
Unbridled coasts 'n' seas

Easefulness is a plague
As inebriating ast venom o poison
Being dead is too similar
Ceaseless relaxation
Contentment be e titanous injury
A hidden torture didn't ya know   to stay sedentary

It's always sweet
habit and lethargy
We cost our offspring their evolution
The birthright to be plucky
n full of the physical capacity
to take on some another opportunity

Taken generations in the making
Can't you see evolution don't take kindly to the lazy and unchanging
We're all specializing too heavily in doing a good nothing
And having worlds so apt for transforming
Doesn't bid well for us listless creat's

We arrive now to a fjord
Whose waters are burnt sienna
And æthers a solid cordovan
Cliffs an earth yellow
The vegetation of umber shrubs   ochre grasses   russet trees
Scattered about in high density
Ann for those high tops lurking o'er the goodly seaway
casting e shadow of copper
As snow would once mantle them
Instead
We find sand in great dunes of sinopia
Burying the lower portions of fat redwoods
that are shooting out through 'em
corkscrewing high into the air
plentisome spiraling tying together
Whilst their roots of kobicha
burrow through mountain dirt
Field drab   fallow   'n' ecru
Springing forth from the base of rock face
Stabbing into the dew which upon the contact turns chestnut
In our raft with its almond planks
'n' olive sail
We can't help but have auburn cheeks
Put against this brown sugar wind
Carting us gently through this stream
For who knows when it breaks into three or two
Or ad infinitum plus
Any sounds good
*****

Yet imagine findin a toad or skink
That none yet ever hast seen
A monster or perhaps some lovely dame or mang o thing
Provinces untouched
Maybe just somewhere everyone has sought
although you haven't
'Tis all new as long as it is ta you

The gods and kings
priests n geeks
They all wanna keep you in a regulated piece
Powers say stay here
Sign out sign in
For everyone's safety we gotta know a couple things
Where you're going
When you're leaving
When you're returning
and why
We need to know o please
Will have to go find ya without these
Disrespectful belittling reasoning

Well I can't live with that
Only onesself   only one's chosen heartfelt
May know their aims roads 'n' keeps
Close borders have e thousand Identifications
          one of each color or specie

                    So castrate sail
                         Boot any vehicle
                                   clip the wings of anything ærial
                    If i to reach the ends of the world
                              Must have to prove my person
               Then it shall be by my courage and my merit
Only to myself and those who earn it
                    Thus go
                    Break fenceline
                    Blast apart a rampart
                    Unloose e great many knots

          They may have binds
But you have mind
               Eyes or perchance feet
                    Levitation
                              Maybe pinions

          May nowt a bilbo ever hold you
     Go   for there is ample outside and moreso

Cincture.

I saw a moth play In the purple roulette
The dance of dreams and their wonder in my toolkit
A tower of vicious appearance obscure logic complete
Leaving but alone the smithereens of a rare and tender power
In e realm where once I lived I listened e royal speak
"Do not pretend to me experience
Thou art inconsequential
and I a potentate"
And though silence first reared
The rebuke came from one near
"Now thyself maybe sans peer here
Perchance your merit is why you keep that honor
Or fear instilled by thine forefathers
Matters not the manner as I see it
For none should rule alone even if they are chosen
Believe all you want in thy own excellence sturdy as uh tower
Though 'twere not for the million councils of a day and the serviles own complaints
Thee would be clueless 'n' base
How poorly you art already an ingrate"

That speech its cost an existence
The long held confidant   patient n capable
Latent frustrations finally confessed
A person for their candor put to inferno and boiling acids churn[18]
Appaling the day any land
crushes verities inconvenience with a gavel 'nd stake

---

18 The punishment described is a popular type of execution in Timo for the disgraced. Conjecture holds that this refers to the same crux event in Thalon's life that drew him off from family and home. Although using what information exists, the victim outlined in this occasion was possibly a fellow member of the Yawn Gens or some other form of loved one from possibly another Aristo-Gens.

The regular criminals
landlords and princes
merchants bureaucrats ministers
Tax o debt collectors
Name 'em whatever

Excess their game
Swanky the look
Luxury tha woo
Cruelly after more too
But they're not lonesome fools
It's imperative they can't resist
an addiction
Ya can't kick it with the thing to abuse is in your view
Could you
and ye don't

The problem be
Temperance don't actually lead to living good
Antonyms really
A full esse with experience wisdom 'n' gusto
Expensive
Costly enough to charge one the very thing they're trying to grow
Risks   heartaches   all your savings
If you want to have an exciting living ya gotta use them
Calculations   statistics
Mathematics divine ast they are
can't figure everything

Calmness 'n' careful they're wonderful in parable
But soon the next instant you want something out of here
Something over there inaccessible even impossible
And that's not wrong
Ya gotta be a maniac
For without even a little lunacy
Without even a itty bitty of fear o fury
I affirm it   die already

*****

We rode now in e river of wine
through a cloudy rainforest
Where giant roses grew
And an oxblood mist reigned
The river dolphins leaping n playing were coquelicot
While the terracotta fish swam in schools so fervently
They stirred the folly mud to the point none could see
beneath such murky red liquidy depths
Yet as one looked closer around
The glints 'n' sparkles all o'er the grounds
Ruby's of all shape shade 'n' cuts stuck out
Turned radiant by cinnabar vines
cutting through the candy red apple high
And upon them were tomato stars shining amaranth rays
That when touching the crystals reflected a cerise hue
Now atop each flower huge
In their comfortable centers
Slept carnelian caterpillars in brick cocoons
That when they wrenched open it was with a fwoosh
Cardinals flew forth upon the wide breeze
Singing songs their notes visible to eye as ear
And one would turn crimson here and heat
As a firestorm builds in the throat
And OUT in a glory of ardour chili pink 'n' maroon
*****

However
Self-gratifying antics as we may task ourselves to undertake
Ast violent rambunctious or blatant we aim
Keep some things cool
A principle if you may
To tolerate
There are those we truly will detest hate 'n' blame
Despise with their pain all the ways
But rather than blanket hubris or rage
Hearken and try (this may sound strange)
Without thinking
(I'll explain)

Withhold judgement and righteousness
Understand why things are said
Hear the wail or yell 'n' reach to touch the bottom of whence it's made
There is always reason tobe proud although never for pomposity
Force breeds ever increased force
If ever anything is wanting for solution
Ya gotta meet it with a straight face a calm mouth
And a head able at digesting
Otherwise tantrums I tell ya they get something done
Yet the results are more harmful than whats won

Listening   who does it harm
Act once good talks are done
By that at least do your part
If the enemy is an idiot then that's their qualm
You're already ahead   they've long lost

Joyitude.

Leave the past for those who lived it
The future still awaits them 'n' thee

Tho' was't by the tardy or patient
fate or destiny dictated

Occasionally joy is rare
Like lightning flare striking the brain
Uncommon the taste
Atypical the state
And instead misery is in turn
A ceaseless torrent
Or just meaninglessness alike tha flood ef e river bank
hard to get rid of
Only able to be outwaited
For no bucket or tool will quicken e change in mood

Jubilee jamboree party
Jubilance is also quite often found in heavy quantity
In drug merry or loving
Friendship bop or adrenaline junkie
Plentiful the fashions to for instants being happy
Multitude a styles to finding satisfaction
Yet this could lead to quite something

Have thou felt high delight
Absolute glee
Tremendous ecstasy
Whether it was by success in passion work or fight
A sudden smile rich
Bright as plasma shining ta blind
but the curved lips open up
And suddenly the teeth have an overcast
The effulgence e farce
Now another magnitude starts up
'n' we go from gleams to gaunt
Then eclipse
Now seethe fume spit
Tempered ire
Outrageous anger
RAGE
RAMPAGE
A monster is let free mid the stage
Swift the movements nothing really gets seen
Then tha speed 'n' wrath are already done
What was just great laughter 'nd fun
Has become a crime scene ann tragedy

AlthoIi have also witnessed that same intensity
Create a masterpiece in but a flurry of strokes 'n' wrote
Save a life   the whole will 'n' body together in beat to a wardrum
'N' still more
Survival the most I've seen
The weights of a thousand giants stacked agin
Beaten back to feel tomorrow's dawn haze
Cooly touch the skin 'nd face again

*****

First off   alabaster sunlight blared
And though what I remember was coming dusk
When the old worlds eye fell
The rise was such
Revealing choruses whose forms
my sight barely could muster
Though I shall try describing what defied my watch
There were strands of flax
Stretching on towards faraway   past the light 'n' horizon line white
The bottom row was filled of virtues dressed in lavender blush
Their weaving filling me of tempest strong ideals
Second were æons of nyanza
Their perpetuity 'n' wisdom drawing my awe
Thirdly the powers who had a platinum hue exuding
Their might and dignity compelling my sense obedient
Fourth were the authorities garbed in bone
Whose coarse look 'n' cunning alighted a deep dread
Fifth the adores in vanilla regalia
Whose magnanimity and compassion gave me feeling
Sixth the passions in armors of azure
Thats boldness 'n' spectacle brought me to understand miracles
Seventh the dreams bedizen in ivory (horn sometimes too)
Whoms beauty n horror arose mine memory with all its details to the prow
Eighth the living attired in misty rose
Whose audacity and obstinance gave me hope
Ninth and with the highest thrones the spirits adorned like ghosts
And when I gazed upon them
Seeing at last truth and certitude
I felt anew
Freedom I found there and knew
And we still upon the raft rose higher than the stage
Higher than the picture
till we were finally sightless

*****

72

Of despondence how could I clown
Agony its vestiges are not proud
Great in scale perchance have you heard a mothers wail
Caused by a host of brews
All from clouts to noose
Poverty to lose
Emotional financial uur just prey te some rouse
The clothes the desks the whole room
'n' village at large completely soused
Despair a horrid bout that must be faced for each death come about
Matched with grief I mean who could hope to last any amount
'Nd this time I can't return with e upside
Anguish is a torture
Down spirits are unbearable
But that is the benefit of them
Sufferings merit is by bearing
Joy within its haste and raze creates happy memorabilia
And woe breaks down the body 'n' brain
That's why it obfuscates
Thus many a time we can't recall what gave us felicity
Then at that point only   by rebuilding are we better
Facing head on the sting 'n' mark of tough luck o hate
New gaiety will raise
However that's not even the focus then
It's about pride in making it out
And breaking even or getting one over 'em
Even though the heavy losing   there's always the opportunity for winning

Septimus.

*****

We come to
And found ourselves
Mid a sea somewhere
That itself was the center of nowhere
'N' the thing to mark the focal point
Was a spire of marble ann stained glass
Who upon the motionless ocean
with o unwavering twilight helping
Layed three images of itself
flat unto the surface
Each a different direction
equally separate
Un its shadow
dual its reflection
Tri a kaleidoscopic version
Stretching far to match the originals height eternal

So to the first step of this tower
With legs   feet   tentacles
We paddle
'Nd for once we step off our vessel
Commencing an upward trudge

Then by a step
We saw plains stretching on
Behemoths grazing alongside buffalo

Thus was as we continued our walk
The changes constant never to stop

We gazed next
At a conifer woodland
Full of brachiosauruses and harpies
That picked the parasites from their enormities

We gazed next
At e volcano in a tundra
Where hydras fought and roared
Whilst caterpillars ignored
All following one another in o row

We gazed next
At a swamp full ef crystals boulders
Here golems moseid
songbirds nesting on their craggy shoulders
lulling stone giants into dancing

We gazed next
At boiling coastlines
Toward the base of cliffs
Whose faces full uf cracks
bled many a different dye
Where sirens lied asleep or weeping
And elephant seals joining them in kind
Yet instead of crying
they bellowed their usual rancors proudly

We gazed next
At dunes in jungles
Where swaned færies outfitted to allure
Ast salamanders warm in the sand
or on pebbles atop puddles napped

We gazed next
At savannas with glaciers carving through
capybaras running around
While gryphons high up roost

We gazed next
At rolling hills
that meteor showers did incessantly haunt
Where moles dug underneath
And will o wisps in e merry
floated everywhere

We gazed next
At rocky deserts
Full of metal monoliths
Each releasing a different colored flame
from their pointed tops
Manticores would drink them dry of their fire
'Nd antelopes would run wild

We gazed next
              at whole worlds
          Coming to 'n' coming apart
      Crashing together growing cold
Wholly altered at the next dawn

      We gazed next
              At solar systems
      Full of things that blew new gusts
                  Cascaded new rains
              Blew up in quaint ways
          All with their own times
      All with their own secrets or lies
All grander than any body can bear uur bind

      We gazed next
              At nebulæ
Beautiful afar ann a irresistible urge to touch
          However tobe near is to die
              The grave n birthplace
  There at the last words or first cries of a star
              Well you would see the heart of life
          But in turn you'd sacrifice thine
                  A worthy price says I

We gazed next now   yet I stopped
Turning roundabout
Back the direction I'd used to rise up
Seeing for an instant plainly   just beauty
Naked galaxies whose centerpieces
their energy staring right at me
Our boat now waited for me
You gotta keep on higher
Deeper into creativity
Going forward into future 'n' dominion lacking a need of me

I can't I've gone the span
I gotta hurry where I'm had
Give back what I can

So I returned to it that miserly raft
Gladder than bliss
Setting off again with almost a blessing lodged in the chest

Digging with a shovel of yen
Through my yon 'n' still toiling for whatever I'm being kept on
Onward togoto an end
*****

Unit.

On the long rocky run
Harpsichords rang aloud in a e fun
Rambunctious vaunt then suddenly none

Sentiment and nous
I'll give a case
To explain the difference betwixt these frames

Spotting a worm in the middle of o path
if you consider it how do you act

Reason orders the bigger creatures passin to pause ann yourself move on

Feeling moves snakish   bugging onto another piece ef sod

We have all set alight highways
Let currents pass us by
Sans so much as a gesture to show ourn recognition
We've each allowed sinkholes 'n' quicksand to consume us
Full and screaming self-pity 'n' prithee
Even though 'twas we that had mortal feet

If you dip straight into disgrace o shame
Wherefrom doth complaints get made

I've often worried of the greater world
No farther on much
Uf enslaved starving 'n' distraught
Never able to comfort anything significant of tha entirety
Wanting to remedy as much ef their problems
Help them with their itty plots for getting along
You'll hand what your own situation will allow thee to hand
However when does respite last
for the one it comes to
'Nd how do we judge 'n' motion
for the twenty more afterward that it does not

Where do we define the line
Between swift action
and asking why

What happens
For when I hear the musics of love 'n' compassions
The joining in of the the crowd
to a musician 'n' singers
Precious lyrics 'n' harmonious lay
They speak then of better days
Light on the way
Beautiful deeds
Everyone feels like a poet when they sing
Yet once melody drains away
Strain dissipates
Shouldn't the message stay
Returning to their lives
Why does forever it take
Even the littlest change to take hold
manifest into the bold
From local to whole
I guess just as among two
True amore is hard 'n' slow to grow

I wonder
When you rule
Is birdsong just another sound in the vacuum

Are love songs too cruel then
Do they feel like a class action or harassment
Why did we stop listening
Why don't we keep the lessons
We just gotta keep singing
Ur find some answers through reason

Cause if we don't
will soon (as ever) be killin'
or sinking

Main.

*****

Give us the truth
Who de we blame
The aged or the youth

Neither
for while you're still kicking
You've got a duty to the living

Nobody carries grace or salvation
it's found through community n caring

You shan't give up the past
Nor silence yours or anothers histories
Though I tell ya each creature is innocent
ef all wrongdoings prior to its existing

From tomes of old in libraries
that their dust won't allow you to breath
Artifacts sealed away within cyclopean architecture
Or stacked atop some grave robber or rich fellas stockpile
From burial grounds to palaces
Abandoned factories 'n' townships
Vehicular graveyards to wastelands
Used up weapon testing sites
Forsaken military bases
Shipwrecks   clay tablets   molded parchments
Moth plagued clothing
Citadels to moat 'n' bailey
O even just your elders stories brought down
From their own sagas   Maybe even older antiquities
Mythology uur te annals of some peoples

These things tha Ancient I shall deem
Slowly show themselves in these present rounds

Ruptured bone
Jugular splitting
Smashed hands
Ripped out nails
Nails driven deep
through palm or sole
A breaking wheel
Tar and feather
Waterboard
Chains Whips
Cattle prods tasers jumper cables
Barbed o razor wire

                              Chevalet
                                Pilliwinks
                                The rack
                            A leg-screw
                      Turkas nd strappado
        Flaying
                        Slow slicing
                          Disembowelment
                                  Crucifixion
                          Impalement
          Crushing stoning
                            Burned at the stake
                                  Boiled to death
                      fed your own digits fried to a crisp
                      Dismemberment
            Sawing
        Scaphism
            Necklacing
                        Decapitation
                          Berate
                              Subjugation
                                      Repression
                        Suppression
                                    Beatings
                            Thrashings
              Whompings
                              weakness
        Depression
                          Anguish agony hate
              Despair grief
                      Rage anger vex
                      Pestering bullying
              Rape murder kidnapping
          Abuse manipulation
    Molestation indoctrination
          Mock execution
      Learned helplessness
Depersonalization
        Psychological regression
            Sensory deprivation
              Thirst hunger starving
                Loneliness separation
                      Destruction devastation
                                  Nightmares
                          Extinction genocide
                Fratricide infanticide deicide
                      Disassociation insanity
                                  Hopelessness

A dying or dead dream
To top it off
Simply
Tears and wailing

These things ta Horror I claim
Rush at us in e violence now

From Ladybugs
to Worms
Ta Bee's
Te Ants
T Beetles
Butterflies 'n' mantes
every bug or insect each one
Lollipops
Jelly beans
gumdrops
Honey Chocolate
Sugar cane
Molasses maple syrup
Sweetened tea
Melon
Long apples or short those even with pines
Orange tangerine mandarine
Plums passion-fruit peaches
Berries grapes
Their many variations
Trees
Covered in deciduous leaves
Bare as can be
Or fuller with life in that green
than perhaps most will ever feel
Grasses from blue to stained with random tints
Golden to teal
Verdure of each look or fit
Shrub ivy mint
Spice and spines
Then flowers floret blooms
Fields to their brim with them
Urr just e bouquet
Need I describe we've seen their million forms
Each wonderful and its own
Birds as well
Animals galore
The natural world   the total
Open sky o fjord or molten core
What then about joy

Happiness praise allure
Friendship Ardour
Family Lovers Lo
Awe Majesty
Greatness magnificence
Modesty honesty
Prayer sanctity
Sanity
Gift giving sharing
Charity helping
Supporting one another
Bravery Quick wittedness
Ambition intelligence
Compassion empathy
Mystery majesty
Dreams
Beauty

These things the sacred I avow
As well came around
Gently towards us all

So what do we do
With everyone of these stuffs put before our face
Our brains to intake Our bodies bear forthwith
Our legs quake our mouths sigh (Is it for love or tiredness)
Our eyes perspiring (miserably o happy)
We take it in
Deeply without a hesitation
and transmutate

The cosmos rules
Innermost to outermost
Nadir to zenith
infinite
Only that which is as such
can take within itself that much

Take it all within
Then do as the divine
Make something of this
Create   cause you can't destroy
only reform it
*****

Great Palisade.

*****
We've approached now to a place
Where the water is still
Colorless and dead
With no wind ever to speak of either
And soon e barriers wide face
rising out from the horizon at e sloth's pace
As we slowly paddle through the expanse
Ta reach its mein

We come to it
So close ya just reach out 'n' touch
Solid and featureless
You look left
Squint even
'N' all ye can see is stretch
Ya peer right
and what you spy is just its continuing on
Down is just plain
What is there to watch
Except your reflection atop blank slop

So then we lay
Staring straight above o'er us
And what is it we saw
There at the cusp
Between here ann unbarred sky
The familiar dust called clouds
Stacked right against the wall
Completely incapable to pass through

Yet what else
For we tend to configure 'n' constrew
These shifting sopping collections
Into that which we know or knew

So what did we see there pooling
impeded by the impenetrable cumber
Our covets 'n' strife
Many a nostalgia aswellas likes
Various animals
Some of mythical stature
Others just alike to you or I
Losses nd sincerity
Wrongdoings then adversity
Self righteousness arrogance
Risks and occasional victories
Sacrifices next rashness

Pride or lessons had
Sadness love's gone
and our will
(Was thine standing or kneeling
Be critical be honest when it concerns
thy own volition
Only that way can it find the strength
tobe straight legged)

And after all these visions
We get a solitary continuous one
Simply just your own visage
In e constant change
Becoming relatives 'n' friends
Close ones nd far
Enemies and stars
Then lastly me
followed by everyone thou barely or never knew

Throughout back to back
End ta end
Ho sign is shining 'nd loud
Written upon is a clear phrase
"No in   None out"

Such as such
What then does it take
To feel a sense of liberty from this state
If we break out eventually life rolls about
Building up another barricade
That's trauma forgetfulness 'n' distrust
That's longing miseries 'n' lies
But don't you think it could also be good experiences
A hierarchy of preference and dislikes
That causes one to shut up to new times
Joyous memory as much a crux as woe and whine
For the more ya stare about
At tha passed glad 'n' damn
The iceberg or tsunami
Will come from bow port or star
Your whole venture done in a smart
Or instead you just won't reach the land
The one not too distant
with your loved ones screaming graces
Yelling beggings
Setting off smoke signals to u
However ur eyes won't turn e glance to another side

Though I can't blame yee
For each instant is different
            Its own unique plights uur cheerfulness
This so consistent
            many already suffered of this blindness
                  Fallen back straight in the very same position

                  So can I answer the question
                  How to escape the reocurring derision

            No   although I can hope you witness it
                  Calling me out when I fall back in
      You gotta have someone on the other side
                                    Or you just gotta fly
                  Yee can make your problems as long as time
                        Make 'em deep as death or void
                                    Sturdy ast reality
      However I believe you can only go so high
            We can climb   ride up   bound atop
                  Again fly   Now you'll see why

The Clouden Sphere.

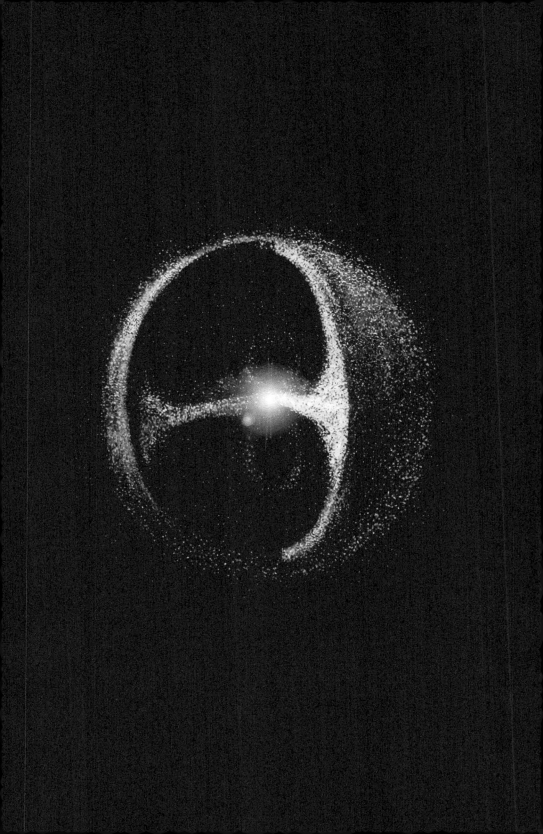

One world
Tens of nations states empires   Borders designating specific space
A hundred towns metropolis villages cities   Places to mill in awhile
A thousand streets walkways roads   Where is meandered   A sort of wilds
A million livings   The routes everyone designates
A billion lives   What more to convey   I don't need to explain
Multiply this by many
And soon we see countless of spirits
Riding their needs 'n' whimsies wheresoever they end up springing
Then of those   How many connect
How many have a meeting with meaning
Who stands by who
Which are each's beloved 'nd true
                     adversaries or doom
But instead of question some individual nobody knew
Something not too unknown by now to you
Lets just listen 'n' watch

                              You walk and eye
                                      Me
                              eye them   eye we

And we   part and separate
Spectator as well ast player
            saw everything
Each nameless and clean slate
Every single of those strangers ann unfamiliar
                    Newcomer   Alien   Visitor
        As you like
Everyone yet conversed with or by some capacity understood
                    These of boundless forms
Mannerisms 'n' characters   limitless modes
        Just see the bustling city street
Hundreds walking forward the hundreds more stepping on backways
                    They as they are

            Yet suddenly pausing
            setting aglow
        Beginning then their shapes to slowly crumble undone unfold
Each one of we   harshly then are heard
            'n' start us to vision
                CRACK CRUSH CRACK
        Then abruptly in the middle of our watching
Like a nightgown getting shrugged
            to display the most blessed and beautiful body
                Out poured from each one
        A flock or more uur even just alone
Of swans hummingbirds storks
        Parrots peacocks geese
            Owls doves finches
                and songbirds galore

                Going
                Rising
            rising into an awesome light
                on unseen breeze
                    breeze without whimsy
                        breeze that breathes for aye and we

Collecting as a host
Into a storms billow
of nothing more than luster and wings
Ann forth from this brilliant nimbus above
Greater pinions dawn
That took on a sleek appearance
Whose tintage stood blazing true
Red-brown outer space with a hint of sunny orange
In each feather 'n' hair that bloomed into view
The nobility shone
drawing wonderment with the revealing of the beak golden
The claws next rousing underneath
Talons of gunmetal inciting a deep dread
Then as the ball of light finished to disappear
Fully in the airs gathering its feeling
The radiance subsided
To reveal its eyes
That stabbed to look on
Sclera of tanzanite blue
Iris of amethyst hue
And a pupil whose circular shape uf a polished garnet tint
Held within a litany of shapes and strings
Dancing together changing shades
singing pæans and hymns

And this creature
This being of them and he
We also she
For in that crowd of eggs   us each were one of them
'Nd in our pure vital vim 'n' vigor
We wheeled

Becoming this

The Falcon
'N' it began to soar
Soaring about in circles then off toward more
Looking to escape the globe
Striding strongly without repose
Giving all its magnitudes to go
For in the clouden sphere
In which we art all ensnared ensorcelled and enclosed
The gales and other forces nonpareil
Resist van or pennon

The beauty of it taking along the ride
Lines of light drawn through an imperious sky
Lifting all fear snide foolhardiness or mire

Now
Once or twice or as many as we'd like
The Falcon has been abused by brutes n blight
Used to inspire conspire ultitized for strife
Unjust unrighteous horrible fights
For beauty itself can be used to increase ones might

Though The Falcon its call
Pure as adoration   a smile   or the spirit
Can roar orotund and indisputable
Baying on high through the mounts low or top
The ringing sound reverberating   resounding
Echoing through forest 'n' rock to the organ of hearing
smiting right through to the heart
'N' the farther in soul hardest to touch
Stirring a fine will   A courageous love
Bellowing forth tha freest song that'd ever been sung
Composed in a single Squawk turned squall

So i recall The Falcon
from east to west
This roaming specter in its best
Had sprung to the sunlight and test
Summoned its wings full of breath
And at the moment approached in speed
It broke free

*****

Unleashed.

Isn't it said that we must keep to the things we speak

Countless hate to think of this
But a good rest is as valuable as life itself

Ensure that those in your passing
can survive it   And always find a lovely memory
To dote on about yee when they're longing
For how cruel to leave an inescapable pang with more sorrow

The last refuge of liberty is the dream
That taken when the mind is compromised
Safeguard these three
fantasy   brain   livin' free
These are the keys
and you can't be unbound if a single one is missing

Harmony in family
Faithfulness in loving
Honesty in friendship
Reminiscence valued highly
A clear objective
the tiny to the biggest
Keep these meaningful things special
Clasp tightly
They're all often made go astray
Wasted easily

Well then

There is a great pool of life somewhere
and I through some accounting error was given more than my share
Me a criminal I didn't return
Keeping for myself all this living that I could bear
Believing now I've been through what I feel must be felt
thus finally I come back to that pond
Giving back the gift mere luck bestowed on one clown

So friend

Have a great love for life
It's the greatest thing that's occurred to any of we
It must be
Since we can't remember a single prior thing
And anything not worth recalling is completely unimportant

Now

It wasn't too long past
that I still felt the riptides of the world coming back together
After being undone by a punch[19]

Nor

Not too long agone I watched separate worlds 'n' peoples battle each other for a spot
'Nd one entity with gleaming wrath fought for the right
yet asudden dissipate like lifted dust
Then alast to spot those very same forces of prior wreck 'n' fray
unify by a beaut voices love[20]

Not too long ago did I see a great uprise start
Where in those times all forms of beings littered the landscapes soughting their liberty
Threatened to be stolen by faraway tyrants or bureaucrats
Leaving comfort filled homes
for roadsides camps and military quarters[21]

Not too long ago I saw e great mover and shaker
Leading his flock of billion birds righteously across globes unfurled[22]

---

19 He is referencing "The NoF Punch." The creation/natural event that brought the entirety of NoF into being. It is veritably impossible that Thalon was born or lived in the time of A.F. (After the Fist)/Uld NoF. There is no proof, and such a claim directly contradicts several historical sources.

20 A summary of Gladiator's history, the capital world of the entire U.G. The Sereni (extinct) was a sapient species that originated there. And the Wise. Lull, who was one of them, during the closing of the period known as B.U. (Before the Union)/Metamorph NoF. Called the Era of Amalgam, she, through her efforts, eventually founded the U.G.

21 Refers to the Apogean War, mainly taking the regularly loathed stance of giving particular regard and seeming agreement with the Entente's reasoning for why they fought. However, 'tis argued 'twas during the Apogean Age when most contemporary sources agree he was born.

22 Ninamore/Nicanore Volée Parca and his Kindred/Brood. He was hailed as a heroic figure by the Entente and served them as a commandant of their military force. Of all foes of the United Governance at that time, he was the most significant threat to the point of being labeled as an arch-villain/threat to the union, for he and the hosts he commanded nigh brought the U.G. to collapse.

And not too long ago did I see the fear that strings can put in all beasts souls[23]

Not too long ago I heard of the discovery of a place
where from every reach 'n' depth   a butterflies wing flaps could be heard[24]

Not too long ago I saw passion and pride stamped out by cruelty and bout

Not too long ago I saw biospheres cultures peoples put to the pyre
And so wast eradicated what holds fast
and so gains those who never witness what loss was had
releshing alone the comforts that sustain their demand
(When conquerors proudly vaunt to play as grace
and fractures at avarice's waiting fangs)[25]

Not too long ago I saw shadows become paisans of rictus and grin
Masking the rotting teeth of fiends
With umbras that only by medals gleamed
Will illusion win[26]

---

23 Refers to Adalfuns Quixyo, an utterly checkered and unrivaled influential figure in U.G. history and still in our time; Currently, the 'Basileus" (Deified-monarch) of the independent world Basilium/Examussium. He, in the Apogean Age, by force through the slaying of the Wise. Aturos took the Seat of Wisdom and led the U.G. to ultimate and total victory in the Apogean War. Furthermore, this line refers to his famed Sensus, a power that seemingly manipulates space and song to his will by playing with strange tethers of reality like some string instrument.

24 Refers to the discovery of Mt. All on the absolute fringe of the Levant Bergen, defining the border with Þe Reign.

25 The exterminations/cleanings: terraforming that created the first generation of reservoir worlds and what would end up with the demise of several Entente world ecosystems and the displacement/eradication of whole peoples and cultures. It was a landmark issue within the U.G. which nearly caused an actual splitting up of the union through a cold war regularly referred to as The Rupture; this period lasted from the winter of the Apogean age into the period known as Pax Unitatus (A.U. 1403-1703F).

26 Rather negatively, he means the founding of the Fulcrum of Confidence. (F.C.) Done so by Wise. Zar-Vohu Ashan, another highly challenged and debated event in U.G. history.

Not too long ago I saw rawest light made to wane
and in turn
wert painted the decaying murals and limp poems bamboozled hands master
So flame fantastic bore forth word
and tears from raze whirled
Where each one that fell shook the planets 'n' stars with resounding yawp
seeking some response[27]

It was not too long ago
that I saw you and you saw me
A moment just as important ast these
no more special   no more irreversible   no less temporal

Now
I muster my courage
For one more selfish step in this dance

Farewell unco and wonted
Worker and bungler
Captain of industry o robber baron
Deluded fantast or incurable wight

Of all us regular foreigners
I only wish of each other we had knew longer
But for what we did compart
I hand my gratitude
to you

---

27 The capture and public execution of Ninamore/Nicanore Volée Parca after his capture by the Tri-directorate of Special affairs & Intelligence (SAI). Many Fet after the Apogean War, one of the worlds destroyed by the exterminations/cleanings was his homeworld of Mouzkⵉn. In response, he committed what is among many an infamous deed regarded as the greatest act of terror and revenge in UG history, "The Crushing of The Helm/Wringing of the Gladiator." Using his legendary Sensus dubbed Push & Pull, he single-handedly set upon the headquarters of the UG with monstrous vivacity, pulverizing the entire Citadel complex and killing an even now unknown number of UG citizens, officials, and honored/notable persons. Including even at the time prior and then-current Seat Holders in the Congregation of Humors.

Future stories from the universes of Lannunival & NoF

Heptad
Simón Berrio-Ariza (Various Authors)
A collection of seven narrative poems from different eras in the kosmos of Lannunival and its consequent universe: NoF. Authors range from Maquereau "The Goon" to Roansol "of Wounds" to Oanærie of Liflär and more.

The Y Scar
Simón Berrio-Ariza (Oanærie of Liflär)
From death to newfound life, a creature bounds forth from his sepulcher to go into the service of a goddess. Who by coincidence has brought about his resurrection after having reconstructed their world. In doing this, he will find a way to regain his memory of that previous life and remedy a corruption, a deformity formed at the outset of this new world, slowly rotting away at this reborn cosmos.

The Tourbillions
Simón Berrio-Ariza (Maxrose "The Goon")
This poetic work was written during his journey when part of the hit squad TOLL on their quest to assassinate an Empyrion of Bizalom during the final stretch of The Rupture period in U.G. History. The product of his altering perception while traveling between worlds and his ultimate revelations during the wild and history-changing conclusion caused by him and his friend to this infamous and tragic era.

The FoxBird (Two Volumes)
Simón Berrio-Ariza
Follows the tale of Abilene upon her dying world of Basilium: A female Basilinem who, after the destruction of her home, goes into the service (as the gardener) of the God-king of her world, the infamous Adalfuns Quixyo. Read as they develop a deep friendship that could perchance tame his waxing madness, and a long-time friend scared for her life risks his own to rescue her. Read how their actions affect the world and may restore it from oncoming ruin through the events in this narrative.

Fire Inducer (Four Volumes)
Simón Berrio-Ariza
This story takes place in some of the earliest periods in the kosmos of Lannunival. Namir: a fire, sets out into the universe venturing through impossible lands, strange peoples, and deadly circumstances as he grows from child to adult. Tackling issues ranging from the simplest to the most complex having encounters even with the very deities of his universe in the name of his quest: to find his brother Mishka.

Wanderings in the Welkin
Simón Berrio-Ariza (Kið. Ein-Clod and Kin. Gins-Sang)
The complete written account of the voyages of Ein-Clod and Gins-Sang while aboard the ship Havo crewed by mercenaries. From their childhood struggling to survive on a colony at the frontiers to end up peerless daredevils and adventurers at odds with nature, foe, and sometimes even friends. While they traverse the most untamed and strange places, making discoveries that would rightfully place them among the pantheon of giant figures during the Renascence period of the United Governance.

Climax of The Seasons (Three Volumes)
Simón Berrio-Ariza
Lannunival undergoes calamity. The universe is set upon by an unstoppable apocalypse, stagnating and freezing the kosmos in a timeless and motionless pause. The emperor of fear in profound desperation seeks any recourse to the all-swallowing catastrophe. Convening with deities and powers to seek out anyone who has a solution as his verse-spanning empire comes apart. However, afar, accompanied by a Heroic band, a newly crowned unexpected character is dubbed the King of Romance as his influence grows and the Emperors' wanes. Their conflict will decide the course of their verse.

The NoF Punch (Five Volumes)
Simón Berrio-Ariza
Concerns the life of Amadio Lator and his rise to fame for his bon vivant, violent, and daring lifestyle: A member of the species Homo Potens he will display all his strength of will, character, and body as he traverses the world, provoking havoc, conflict, and getting vengeance for many a downtrodden person everywhere he goes. In the wake of this, another inspired by Amadio will rise to prominence, his arch-rival and dearest friend Adalfuns Quixyo the perpetual villain of the world to come. Watch as these two struggle, and cause havoc worldwide, amounting to an accident of Kosmic implications, bringing to an end the verse of Lannunival and inciting NoF.

Apogee
Simón Berrio-Ariza
Chronicles the life and times of Nicanore Volée Parca, starting with his origins as an orphan in the world of Moksan. Until his prominence as a commandant of the military forces of The Entente during the Apogean War. Afterward, turning pirate and terrorist, seeking vengeance, causing untold horror and slaughter for the destruction of his world and people. Until his self-sacrificial execution and heralded last words.

All are Yours
Simón Berrio-Ariza
Ancient and cherished tale of the Færirkið of Svaki, following the ludicrous adventures of the semi-historical/semi-legendary grand patriarch of the Mikos family: Miko Parisio. Accompanied by his valiant compatriot Orlando Rohan "The Goblin." Assailing onward so that Miko may bed the princess of Pandemonium Aleasia de Sonrisas, already the wife of the dauntless Potent-ante-Markgraf de Los Humores: Adolphus Timur Maldoror. Read as they risk health and sanity while provoking upheaval throughout their nation, all to satisfy Mikos's desire.

Mikossaga
Simón Berrio-Ariza
Semi-sequel though mostly a historical record, follow the tumult and enlightenment caused by multiple generations of the Mikos family. How they unified the world of Svaki and birthed universal democracy—helping to bring their world to the space age. Then how the last member of the family, through their self-sacrifice. Proved essential in repelling an invasion of Svaki by the people of Serenus while led by the enigmatic and titanic persona known as Þe Gladiator.

The Onpaisfyst
Simón Berrio-Ariza (Aynmois "La Wyrm")
The biography and philosophy of one of the first greats of the Renascence period of U.G. history: Lea-Non "The Regginbow." Who by accident destroyed his homeworld and discovered the Onpaisfyst phenomena. Then dodging execution at the hands of the authorities of the U.G. founded the first monasteries based on the way of life he developed from all his experiences and eventual mastery of the power.

The World Gnarled
Simón Berrio-Ariza (Jeroak E. Protozoan)
Tells of the closing times of The Rupture, revealing a U.G.-spanning conspiracy leading to the deaths of many prominent figures of the time. All to end the long-standing and continuously escalating cold war between the several member powers of the United Governance. While sharing the actual lives and actions of the primary perpetrators, the assassin, thief, and poet who composed the infamous hit squad TOLL.

Silver & Robins
Simón Berro-Ariza
Accounts the entirety of the adventures of the peerless Robin and Silvær as the latter seeks to fulfill his childhood dream and the other is ever trying to find his. Across all of NoF, their antics will take them against everyone and everything that would keep them from their ambitions. Even to the point of challenging all the most extraordinary powers of their world as they go gallivanting from place to place on endless escapades. Participating in and provoking a slew of historical events one after the other, sundering and evermore transforming their world.

Ganu "The Impossible"
Simón Berrío-Ariza
Long after the ending of the Annals of Romance and Fear, Lannunival is left hopeless and spiritless. An unimportant and ordinary creature because of a strange event that occurs to him while on a hunt. Gets mutated, his home and country obliterated, and his mind rendered absolutely insane. Mad, he designs an unbelievable project to rejuvenate the world through the redemption, denouncement, and revival of the elemental powers of the universe with the accomplishing of ten feats.

Annals of Romance and Fear
Simón Berrio-Ariza
After the events of Climax of the Seasons, read about the stories and histories of Lannunival. Involving the unending feuds and continuous conflicts between the Emperor of Fear, the forces, deities, and the subsequent Kings & Queens of Romance aided by the remnants of the original Heroic Band.

Made in the USA
Middletown, DE
26 February 2023

25575063R00066